Good Morning, Groundhog!

by ABBY KLEIN

illustrated by
JOHN McKINLEY

SCHOLASTIC INC.
New York Toronto London Auckland
Sydney Mexico City New Delhi Hong Kong

To Ryan and Sabrina, two really great kids!
Love,
—A.K.

To Kathleen with thanks,
—J.M.

ISBN: 978-0-545-14177-2

12 11 10 9 8 7 6 5 4 3 2   10 11 12 13 14 15/0

Printed in the U.S.A.   40
First printing, January 2010

"Tomorrow is a special day," said Mrs. Wushy. "Does anybody know what it is?"

“It’s Valentine’s Day!” yelled Max.

“No, it’s not!” said Chloe.

“Yes, it is!” said Max. He stomped his feet.

“I know what tomorrow is,” said Robbie. “It’s Groundhog Day.”

Chloe held her nose.
"Groundhogs are dirty and stinky," she said.
"I think groundhogs are cute," said Jessie.
"What is Groundhog Day?" I asked.

"A groundhog sleeps inside a hole all winter," said Mrs. Wushy. "On Groundhog Day, he comes out and looks around."

Mrs. Wushy continued. “If he sees his shadow, people think there will be six more weeks of winter,” she said.

“What if he does not see his shadow?” asked Jessie.

“That means spring is coming,” said Mrs. Wushy.

“Spring has to come soon,” said Robbie. “I want to play baseball.”

“I will know before any of you,” I said.
“How?” said Max.
He stuck his nose in my face.

“A groundhog lives under my porch,” I said. “I named him Gary. I am going to get up early tomorrow. I will wait for him to come out of his hole.”

After school, Robbie came over to my house for a sleepover.

"Where is the groundhog?" asked Robbie.

"Under the porch," I said.

"Can I see it?" asked Robbie.

"Sure," I said.

“I just have to get a flashlight,” I said.
“Why?” asked Robbie.
“It is very dark under the porch.”
I grabbed my shark head flashlight.

We ran down the stairs.

"Where are you boys going?" called my mom.

"To see Gary," I shouted.

"Who is Gary?" asked my mom.

"The groundhog who lives under the porch," I said.

"Why do you need a flashlight?" asked my mom.

“We want to shine it down Gary’s hole,” I said.

“We want to see if he has a shadow,” said Robbie.

“I do not think that is a good idea,” said my mom. “I think you should leave him alone. He needs to rest. Tomorrow is his big day.”

“Can I just show Robbie where the hole is?” I asked.

“Okay,” said my mom. “Wait for me. I want to go with you.”

We ran outside with my mom.

"Do not touch the hole," she said.

Robbie and I got down on our hands and knees and crawled under the porch.

“It’s dark under here,” said Robbie.

“I know,” I said. “It’s cold, too! I hope Gary is warm and cozy down in his den.”

We crawled around a little bit more.
“Do you see the hole yet?” asked Robbie.
“I found it!” I yelled.

“I don’t hear anything,” Robbie whispered. “He is still hibernating.”

“I hope he wakes up tomorrow,” I said.

“It is his big day!” Robbie said. “Of course he is going to wake up.”

“See you tomorrow, Gary,” we said.

"Mom, can we get up early tomorrow morning to look for Gary?" I said.

"Dad has to go with you," said my mom.

"He will have to get up extra early," I said.

"We do not want to miss Gary," said Robbie.

It was still dark when I shook my dad.

"Wake up! Wake up! It is time to go!"

"Go where?" asked my dad.

"We have to see if Gary sees his shadow!" I said.

My dad put on his bathrobe and slippers.
Robbie and I ran downstairs.
"Come on, Dad! Hurry up!" I yelled.

We ran outside.
"It is freezing out here," I said.
"I feel like a Popsicle," said Robbie.
We did a little dance to stay warm.

I heard a little squeak.
Gary ran out from under the porch.
"Good morning, Gary," I called.

Gary looked around.
He did not see his shadow.

“No shadow! No shadow!” Robbie and I sang. “Thanks, Gary. Spring is almost here!”